D0871466

THE AVENGERS

VISIT US AT
www.abdopublishing.com

Reinforced library bound edition published in 2011 by Spotlight, a division of the ABDO Group, 8000 West 78th Street, Edina, Minnesota 55439. Spotlight produces high-quality reinforced library bound editions for schools and libraries. Published by agreement with Marvel Characters, Inc.

Printed in the United States of America, Melrose Park, Illinois.
042010
092010
This book contains at least 10% recycled material.

Library of Congress Cataloging-in-Publication Data

Tobin, Paul.
Don't follow the leader / story, Paul Tobin ; art, Horacio Domingues.
p. cm. -- (The Avengers)
"Marvel."
ISBN 978-1-59961-767-1
1. Graphic novels. I. Domingues, Horacio, ill. II. Avengers (Comic strip) III. Title.
PZ7.7.T62Don 2010
741.5'973--dc22

2009052833

All Spotlight books have reinforced library bindings and are manufactured in the United States of America.

CENTRAL PARK, N.Y.C.
Here's the rules. We race each other through Central Park. No tripping. No tackling. No tickling.
And whoever wins gets these front row tickets to the United States versus Japan All-Star baseball game.

Exactly. And you can't use your webbing.
Yes, I can. And you can't throw things at me.
But I will. Ready?
Oh yeah.
On the count of three.
One!
Two!
WEEET WEEET WEEET
Wait! My phone!
Seriously? Your phone? Is this some spider-trick?
Shush.

What's going on?
Some guy pleading for help. Says he's been kidnapped. Forced to commit a crime.

They're making me steal things from an army base!
Is this for real?

Let me get this straight...at this very moment you're sneaking onto an army base?
Sneaking?

SPIDER-MAN
TIGRA
STORM
WOLVERINE
LUKE CAGE

No. We're not exactly *sneaking*.

DON'T FOLLOW THE LEADER

PAUL TOBIN WRITER

HORACIO DOMINGUES PENCILER

CRAIG YEUNG INKER SOTOCOLOR COLORS
DAVE SHARPE LETTERER JONES & SOTO COVER
PAUL ACERIOS PRODUCTION RALPH MACCHIO CONSULTING
NATHAN COSBY EDITOR JOE QUESADA EDITOR IN CHIEF
DAN BUCKLEY PUBLISHER ALAN FINE EXECUTIVE PRODUCER

MARVEL®
Spotlight

TWO HOURS LATER.
OUT
So, some of the soldiers we talked to said the Rhino was a part of this, and some of them said he wasn't.
And most of them gave me their phone numbers.
Me too.

It's actually rather hard to tell how *much* of a part the Rhino played in this attack.
You'll see what I mean in these *tapes.*

"Look here. The Abomination is busting through the outside wall, and there's the Rhino right behind him.

"But here the Rhino is saving two of my men from the Leader.

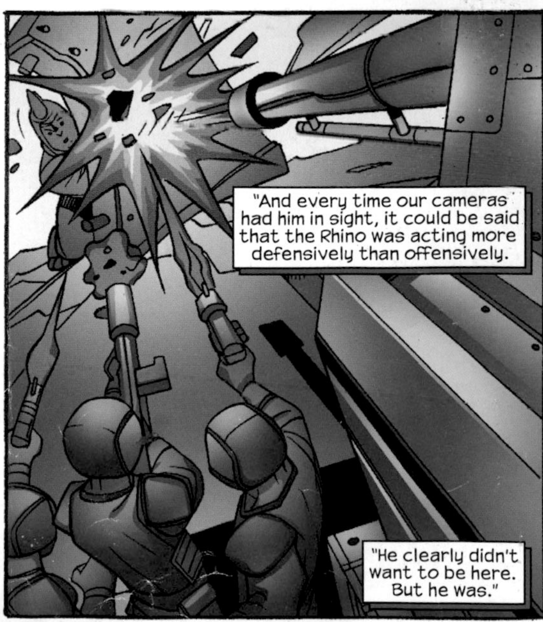
"And every time our cameras had him in sight, it could be said that the Rhino was acting more defensively than offensively.
"He clearly didn't want to be here. But he was."

You say the Rhino called you to say he was being *coerced?*
Yep. Kidnapped. Forced into a *life of crime.*
Of course, he was *already* leading a life of crime, so we're a bit *confused.*

What *purpose* did the Leader have in attacking this base?
Ohhh, I'm not sure. Maybe nothing. Maybe just to stir up trouble?

Wrong. Maybe the *Abomination* thinks *beating up army bases* is a cool hobby, but the *Leader* is a man with a *purpose.*
He wanted something. What was it?
I'm afraid that information is *classified* under the federal--

You *kidding* me? I have *Avengers* level access.
I'm authorized to know *anything* and *everything,* from what *underwear* you put on this morning to *whatever it is* that the Leader stole, so save me a *phone call* and tell me the *truth.*
The truth about the *Leader, not* that *under-wear* thing.

OR

If you *think* you can come onto a *U.S. Army base* and threaten *me* with--
BEEP
BOOP
BIP
Ahhh, *dang.* What a *day.* It was *satellite codes.*

tellite es? The r isn't going messing with satellite elevision, is he?
Because the World Sumo Championships are--
We're talking military satellites. Secret ones.

And these secret military satellites, what do they do?
Well, there are several of them, and they each have lasers.
And these lasers, how powerful are they?

Not too powerful. At least, not unless they're combined.
Yeah. It is.
This is where you tell us the Leader can combine them now, isn't it?

"With all of the codes the Leader now has, he could, umm, align them into a single laser capable of wiping out... oh...a small town."

A small town? The laser could blast a small town?
And what is your definition of a small town?
Oh. Umm. Ahh...about the size of maybe... Chicago?

Did he just say Chicago?
Yes. I fear that he did.

So we have a huge laser in the sky, and it's now controlled by a mad genius and two of the world's strongest villains, although one of them claims to be kidnapped.
Why do I always get these jobs?
Because Iron Man hogs all the missions with rainbows and winged puppies.
Dang!

Wolverine, I hope you're finding something, because getting this general to talk is like pulling candy-coated teeth from a baby.

Yeah. I found something interesting just sorta lying around in a vault.
Grab it. We'll meet you back at the Quinjet.

SOON. IN THE QUINJET.
What did you find?
Looks like ham sandwiches. Turkey sandwiches. Roast beef sandwiches. Jeez, even olive loaf.
Yeah...I snuck in a little trip to the commissary. Some good eating.

But chomp your eyes on this.
Whoa. These are schematics for the laser array.
Chomp your eyes on this? What does that even mean?

The Leader must know he's on a tight deadline. The access codes are difficult to reset, but it shouldn't take more than a day.

That means he has to make his move soon.
He'll be-- ahh! I see how this works.

Storm. I've got an important job for you.
Of course. Just tell me what you wish.

ONE HOUR LATER.
So how do we find the Leader?
WESTMINSTER'S
And how do we find a better hot dog? This one tastes like a donkey.

Finding the Leader could prove problematic. Next to Reed Richards, he's probably the smartest man alive.
Right. And that makes him good at hiding.
If I cooked hot dogs like this, I'd go into hiding.

Good thing you have this umbrella.
Yeah. It's getting cloudy. Wasn't it supposed to be sunny all day?
And hot dogs are supposed to taste good. Know what I'm sayin'?
Jeez, Wolverine... didn't you just eat about half that army base's rations?

My mutant healing factor makes for a fast metabolism. I get hungry. Got a problem with that?
Gosh no, Mr. Scary Man. And these hot dogs taste fine to me.

Are you demented? I could do a better job cooking these things! A schnauzer could do a better job! An insect! Even Spider-Man!
I think I was insulted somewhere in there.
Yeah. Let's mess with him.

I bet you twenty dollars Spider-Man can cook a better hot dog than you.
You're on! Hand me the spices and stand back!

I'll take two.
Two, please.
Can he wear the apron?

CLICK CLICK CLICK
I'm having Iron Man track down all suspicious sales of tech equipment. Hopefully we can chase down the Leader that way.
I've got feelers out to some of my underworld contacts. Somebody will know some-thing.

You have underworld contacts?
A couple ex-boyfriends. They were nice back when I was dating them.
I'd best reserve comments.

So how 'bout them hot dogs? Pretty good, eh? Now it's your turn, Spidey.
I'll pass. You win.
I just can't take the chance of my friends taking photos of me wearing an apron and putting them online, the way we're going to do with you.
Huh?

You know I'm going to get back at you guys for this.
What can I say? I live for the present.

And speaking of the present, we need to deal with the Leader. Let's get a plan, people. It's not like the bad guys are going to give us a call and tell us what's up.
SHRING
SHRING
Whoop. My phone.
EEP
EEP
Ooo. Mine too.

Hmmm.

I always feel so left out when friends are talking on cell phones.
I could give you a call, if it would make you feel better.

That was one of my admirers from the army base. According to him, they just received a call from the Leader.
He's demanding a quarter trillion dollars, or he'll devastate New York.
That is not good.
My call was from the Rhino. He wants us to know he's not a part of this, and he's currently uploading all the information on where they are, and what they're doing.
We can stop this.
And that is good.

There are three different locations.
Probably a redundancy factor, so that if any one of them gets taken down, then the threat remains.

That means we'll have to take down all three of them.
Luke, you and Wolverine stop the Abomination.
Can do.
Can at least try.

I'm off to take down the Leader!
Be careful!

Okay. I guess I'll just take on the Rhino all by myself then.

THIRTY MINUTES LATER.
Wolverine! I can't keep him away from the laser satellite's trigger device!
Get your claws over here!

I can't even get close to him!

You guys are just too precious!
You wanna fight with the Abomination, you should 'a brought the Hulk!

I mean, what is this? A dainty punk and a runt with ice picks for knuckles?
Wolverine's got more than ice picks.

Yeah? What else?
Well, he's real sneaky. He stole the satellite trigger when you weren't looking.
That I did.

Wha...?

Give that back!
And another thing Wolverine has--

--is a metal skeleton made of the hardest substance in the known universe!
Huh?

Hey!

Oommpf!
Uhhnnn!

The metal is called *Adamantium*.

It hurts, *don't* it?
THUMMPTT

You *could* have let me in on this little *battle strategy* of yours.
Oh. *Sorry.* Is it *too late*?
Because if *not*...then, *hey*... would you mind me *using* you like a *clu* to take down the *Abomination*?
Sure. Why *not* Whatever *works*.

OWNTOWN.
I just don't see how this is going to work.
So! You've gained the Power Cosmic? Then I have no chance!
But still... I'll fight on! The Rhino never quits!
Huh? What are you talking about?

Oooff!
Got you! Now, despite you having harnessed the power of a million exploding suns, despite how you have summoned this fierce thunderstorm, the Rhino will triumph!
Have you gone insane?

Work with me here. I want out of the villain business. No long-term gain, and I feel like a jerk hurting people.
But...if this is going to be my final battle, I'd at least like to go out with a bang.
Oh. I get it. Don't want to get beat up by a tiny ol' girl, huh?

Uhh, yeah. Sorry. I got an image to protect. I was hoping you guys would send the Hulk.
Well, maybe not the Hulk. Let's say... Spider-Man.
At least you've got this storm. That makes for a dramatic fight. Now, okay, let me go on the count of three.
One... two, and...

Tigra breaks free!
No mere mortal can hold this child of the stars!
No! This can't be!

Now you will pay a dire price for challenging the very daughter of the universe!
Arrgh! Such power!
THOOONT

How am I doing?
Not bad. You sound a bit like a hippie, though.
Oooo. Sorry. You ready for the knockout blow?
Yep. Go.

It's clobberin' time!
KWUUMPFF

Tigra, this is Luke. Everything going okay, there?
For sure! Won the fight. Stole a line from the Thing.
I'm totally a hero, and everything's fine.
Except for this rain. I hate it when my fur gets wet.

NEW YORK SHIPYARDS.
My sensors tell me that I am now the last of the three. As ever, the Leader stands alone.
Well, alone except for that rockin' battle suit you made. Don't suppose you'd take it off and really stand alone, would you?

Yow! Okay, okay!
Well, I don't suppose that thing short circuits in the rain, does it?
ZREEEEEEN

Rain? This exoskeleton is capable of complete submersion!
This storm is indeed fierce, but my armor could withstand far worse extremes! It could--
Right. Right. I got it. You don't need to do the full sales pitch. I'm not trying to buy the thing!

Not unless you take it off and let me have a test drive!
Fool! You joke while New York hangs by a thread!

Surrender at once, or I will trigger the satellite laser array, and New York will pay the price.

You know I can't do that.
You have no choice.

You're right. I don't have a choice. There's no way I can let you walk away from here.
I won't do that.

You say that I'm joking while New York hangs by a thread, but listen to me, understand what I'm saying.

I'm not joking.
You're not walking away from here.

Spider-Man?
Stay back. I KNOW what I'm doing.
Ahh, the rest of your team arrives. So be it.

They are just in time to witness the cataclysm. With one click, half of New York will vanish.
The half that I'm not in, of course.

CLICK

Why...why did it not work?

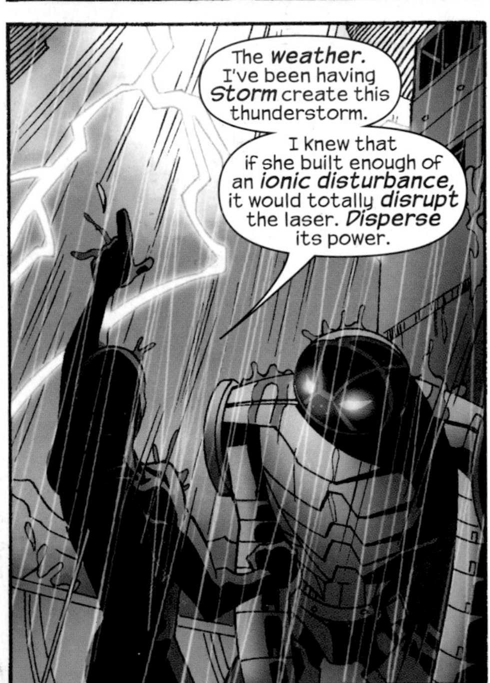

The weather. I've been having Storm create this thunderstorm.
I knew that if she built enough of an ionic disturbance, it would totally disrupt the laser. Disperse its power.

Simply put, I outsmarted you. And I beat you. All thanks to Storm.

KRAAAKKOOOOOOOOM
You've met Storm, haven't you?

How's all your high tech equipment working now, smart guy?
My circuits! They're all fused! I can't move! I'm helpless!
Yeah. We're mean that way.

Great work with the storm, Storm.
Thank you. Shall I let the skies clear now?

Yeah! Because Tigra and I still need to race to see who wins the baseball tickets!
First one back to Avengers Tower wins!
You're on!

Who do you think will win?
Doesn't matter much.

I stole the tickets from Spider-Man. They're mine now.
I told you guys I'd get you back.

ONE DAY LATER.